I SPY WITH MY LITTLE EYE

I SPY GREEN IN THE JUNGLE

Written by
Amy Culliford

Illustrated by
Srimalie Bassani

A Blossoms Beginning Readers Book

CRABTREE
Publishing Company
www.crabtreebooks.com

Level 1 Early Emergent Readers Grades PK-K
Books at this level have strong picture support with carefully controlled text and repetitive patterns. They feature a limited number of words on each page and large, easy-to-read print.

Level 2 Emergent Readers Grade 1
Books at this level have a more complex sentence structure and more lines of text per page. They depend less on repetitive patterns and pictures. Familiar topics are explored, but with greater depth.

Level 3 Early Readers Grade 2
Books at this level are carefully developed to tell a great story, but in a format that children are able to read and enjoy by themselves. They feature familiar vocabulary and appealing illustrations.

Level 4 Fluent Readers Grade 3
Books at this level have more text and use challenging vocabulary. They explore less familiar topics and continue to help refine and strengthen reading skills to get ready for chapter books.

School-to-Home Support for Caregivers and Teachers

This book helps children grow by letting them practice reading. Here are a few guiding questions to help the reader with building his or her comprehension skills. Possible answers appear here in red.

Before Reading:
- What do I think this story will be about?
  - I think this story will be about a spy exploring a rainforest.
  - I think this story will be about finding the color green.

During Reading:
- Pause and look at the words and pictures. Why did the character do that?
  - I think the spy is looking for the color green because he is on a mission.
  - I think the spy swung on the vine to get away from the crocodile.

After Reading:
- Describe your favorite part of the story.
  - My favorite part was when the spy found all the green bugs.
  - I liked seeing all the green trees.

I see green!

I see green trees.

I see a green frog.

I see green bugs.

I see a green crocodile!

What do you see that
is green?

WRITING PROMPTS

Possible answers appear here in red.

1. **Write a different ending to the story.**

The spy gets lost in the rainforest and feels very scared. Luckily, the bugs and birds help him find his way back out.

2. **Choose a character and write the story from that character's point of view.**

The crocodile was hungry and saw a spy that looked delicious! When the spy made it safely across the river, the crocodile had to find something else for lunch.

3. **Write about a similar situation that you experienced.**

My friend and I explored a forest in my backyard. We found all kinds of different bugs and birds! They had many different colors.

ABOUT THE AUTHOR

Amy Culliford has been involved in the arts her entire life. After completing a Bachelor of Fine Arts degree at the University of Victoria, she worked for several years as a drama teacher in classrooms and after school programs. Presently, Amy works for a professional opera company by day, writes children's books by night, and performs as a princess at children's birthday parties on weekends. If she has any spare time, she likes to spend it planning her next trip to Disneyland!

ABOUT THE ILLUSTRATOR

Srimalie Bassani was born in 1986 and lives and works in Mantova, Italy. Her mother gave her a passion for drawing and painting and always encourages her artistic expression. Srimalie attended the Academy of Fine Arts and was later selected for a Master's Degree in Illustration Editorial, "ARS in FABULA," in Macerata.

Srimalie's work is always full of surprises. She likes to diversify her style based on the story she is illustrating, and enjoys drawing in pencil, and then applying color with a graphic tablet. Since 2012, she has illustrated for various publishers.

I SPY WITH MY LITTLE EYE

I SPY

GREEN **IN THE JUNGLE**

Written by: Amy Culliford
Illustrations by: Srimalie Bassani
Art direction and layout by: Rhea Wallace
Series Development: James Earley
Proofreader: Janine Deschenes
Educational Consultant: Marie Lemke M.Ed.

Library and Archives Canada Cataloguing in Publication

CIP available at Library and Archives Canada

Library of Congress Cataloging-in-Publication Data

CIP available at Library of Congress

Crabtree Publishing Company

Printed in Canada/052021/CPC20210520

www.crabtreebooks.com   1-800-387-7650

Published in the United States
Crabtree Publishing
347 Fifth Avenue, Suite 1402-145
New York, NY, 10016

Published in Canada
Crabtree Publishing
616 Welland Ave.
St. Catharines, ON, L2M 5V6

16